For:
Tomas

I hope you enjoy reading
Sam's story.

Sam's

Future Awaits

love,

Daisa ♡

The Magical World of

Fingley

A Storybook World That's Brought To Life!

Sam's

Future Awaits

Daisa Morgan

Daisa & Co
· EST. 2003 ·

DAISA & CO
Lake Village, Far Ings Road, Barton upon Humber
North Lincolnshire, DN18 5RG, England

First published in Great Britain in 2015 by Daisa & Co

Written by Daisa Morgan
Assisted by Jade Smith
Copyright © DAISA MORGAN 2015
Text copyright © Daisa Morgan 2015. All rights reserved.
Original Illustrations by Taryn Shrigley

ISBN 978 0 9567066 8 3

A CIP catalogue record for this book is available from the British Library.

Book typeset by:
DAISA & CO
www.daisa-co.com

Printed in England

Daisa & Co are passionate about helping to preserve the world's remaining ancient
forests. This book is made from paper certified by the Forestry Stewardship Council
(FSC). An organisation dedicated to promoting responsible management of forest
resources.

Dedicated to my much loved grandchildren.

If you want your children to be
INTELLIGENT, read them *fairytales.*
If you want them to be MORE INTELLIGENT,
read them more fairytales.
- Albert Einstein

This book belongs to:

....

Contents

The Magical World of Tingley

A Storybook World That's Brought To Life!

CAREFREE DRIVE

RAINBOWS END

HAZEL & OAK WOOD

SWAN LAKE

AURA'S STABLE

WINDY RIDGE

THE FIELD OF DREAMS

BLUEBIRD BAY

THE FILTER CRITTER

ELF CREEK

ATLANTICUS

GREDNOR

DOLPHIN BAY

BUMBLEBEE CROSS

COBBLESTONES

THE VEGETABLE
GARDEN

DAISY MOUNTAIN

TRADING POST

THE TRADING POST

CRYSTAL CAVE

THE BOUTIQUE

ECO HOUSES

PIXILETA COVE

N

W   E

S

How it all began...

Far away beyond the Universe, Galaxies and Constellations that you see twinkling above you in the night sky, is a wonderful eco world called The Magical World of Fingley.

This is a timeless world, surrounded by golden light where The Fingley Folk, a community of Humans, Faeries, Pixies and other curious creatures live.

It's also the home of a time-travelling bear named Dodl, who used to live in The Great Bear Constellation. In order for Dodl to travel through time and into dreams, Orb the Wizard Bear initiated him into The Pilot Wizard School by holding a special amethyst crystal and asking him to repeat the magic words.

Crystalis, Inspiratus, Amulatus, Travelatum.

Immediately Dodl was astonished to find that his paws had turned purple! When Dodl met Sam and invited him on an incredible night time adventure it led to a life-changing opportunity for him.

Now let the Time Travelling begin…

1

The Weekend Away

The hours and minutes were slowly ticking by. Sam was impatiently tapping his pen on his exercise book, completely disinterested as he constantly checked the hands on the school clock. He was willing them to move faster to signal 'home time'.

At last it was Friday afternoon, but not just any old Friday afternoon. This particular Friday was a special day because tonight, Sam and his family were spending the weekend in their cottage by the coast.

The geography lesson was dragging on for ages and although Sam usually looked forward to these sessions, today the tutor, Mr Taylor was sounding really boring.

He was explaining the different layers of the atmosphere. Then he told the class they were to draw an example of these layers for their homework assignment.

At exactly 3:30 pm ~ the school bell sounded.

It was the end of the day's session and the beginning of Sam's much awaited weekend!

"At last," groaned Sam to his friend Greg.

"I thought this lesson was never going to end! I don't know how I'm going to manage to do my homework because I'm going away for the weekend. Still, I suppose I can ask Dad to help me to finish it when we get back ready to hand in on Monday morning."

"Lucky old you Sam," said Greg. "I'm not going anywhere. I expect I'll have to help Dad with the garden."

Once class was dismissed, the clattering and banging of desk lids could be heard out along the corridor.

Mr Taylor's voice boomed out to quiet them all.

"Quiet please! No running along the corridor, and keep to a single file."

Sam hurriedly pushed his homework and pencil case into his school bag and rushed out of the classroom. He quickly grabbed his coat from the cloakroom and ran as fast as his legs would carry him out of the school gates. He decided to take the short cut across the playground and out along the playing field. Sam's Mum told him that morning that he was to hurry straight home from school because the family would be leaving for the coast shortly after tea time.

All of his thoughts were now totally centred on the coming few days, and how much fun he was going to have. Sam's parents had promised that this weekend they would definitely be taking him to the cottage with his twin sisters Amy and Jessica. Sam was already planning the things he was going to take along with him: his remote controlled plane, his fishing rod, his kite and of course his football.

By the time Sam reached his house, he was practically out of breath. Puffing and panting he dashed through the garden gate and as the gate 'clanked' shut, he accidently trapped his school bag in it.

"Oh no, now look what I've done. Mum won't be very pleased with me," he muttered to himself.

Because he was in so much of a hurry to get into the house, the garden gate had squashed his school bag and torn it on a small nail that was sticking out at the side. As he hurried along the driveway he noticed something unusual ~ his Dad's car wasn't parked in front of the garage as it should have been.

"Oh, Dad's not here. I bet he's gone to the supermarket for food for the weekend," he said. Bursting with excitement, Sam opened the front door, shouting at the top of his voice;

"Mum, I'm home." There was no reply.

"Mum, I'm home!" Sam shouted again.

He stopped to take off his coat and quickly hung it on the coat peg in the hallway, then charged into the kitchen to see if his Mum was in there. Not finding her in the kitchen Sam dashed into the sitting room. As he pushed the door open he stopped dead in his tracks!

Instead of his Mum sitting with the twins on her knee, it was his Granny!

"Hello Sam," she smiled.

"Have you had a good day at school?"

Sam completely ignored her question and snapped back at her;

"Where's Mum?"

"Oh, I'm really sorry Sam, your Mum and Dad have asked me to come and look after you and the twins for a while, because something unexpected has happened at work and they have had to stay behind to sort things out."

Sam looked stunned.

"But they can't stay over at work. We're all going to the coast tonight. Mum especially told me this morning not to be late home from school," said Sam gloomily.

"So because she asked me not to be late, I've run as fast as I can all the way home. I've been looking forward to home-time all day." Sam was really disappointed.

"Well sometimes Sam these things happen, they can't be avoided. But I'm sure everything will be alright," answered Granny.

Sam stamped his foot angrily.

"No they won't!" he shouted.

Sam marched up the stairs, stomping loudly on each one, then 'BANG!'

He slammed his bedroom door shut after him. Sam's Granny thought it best to let him calm down a bit before trying to speak with him again.

She buckled the twins in their buggy and after a short while she went upstairs and knocked on Sam's bedroom door.

"Can I come in Sam please?" she asked.

There was no answer, but she could hear Sam quietly sobbing. Granny opened the door and walked into his bedroom, trying her best to console him.

Sam was lying face down on his bed. His head was plunged deeply into his pillow.

"It's always happening Granny," said Sam tearfully.

"We never seem to have fun these days because Mum and Dad always have to work."

Sam's Granny sat on the edge of the bed beside him. He sat up and she put her arms around him to give him a reassuring hug.

"I know it must seem like that sometimes Sam," she said holding him closely.

"But if they didn't go to work, then you probably wouldn't be able to have a cottage to enjoy anyway."

Sam looked up at her sadly.

"But Granny, all my other friends have fun with their parents, mine just seem to work all the time."

Sam was really upset as his hopes about the weekend were fading fast now.

He looked up at Granny for consolation; his sad blue eyes were moist with tears.

"I'll tell you what Sam, why don't you go and wash your hands and face and get changed from your school clothes?" she said sympathetically.

"Perhaps then we could go for a walk to the park with the twins to get an ice cream. Would you like to do that? By then we might have heard from your Mum and Dad. I'll take my mobile phone with me just in case."

Sam looked back at Granny and with the back of his hand wiped the tears away from his cheeks. He knew that she was trying to be really kind and he loved her lot, but going for a walk to the park to get an ice cream with the twins was no substitute for going to the seaside.

Not one bit!

Sam shrugged his shoulders and blew his nose.

"Ok. I guess so," he muttered, putting his handkerchief back into his pocket.

"We might as well, what else is there to do? But when do you think Mum and Dad will be back?" he asked sadly, still hoping there was some chance of rescuing the weekend.

"Well perhaps it won't be until after you've gone to bed now Sam," she said caringly.

"But never mind, I can put the twins to bed and look after you all until they come back. Let's wait and see what happens."

By now Sam was feeling even grumpier. He changed from his school clothes into his jeans and t-shirt. He looked at his kite that was hanging mournfully on the back of the bedroom door.

"That won't be going flying any time soon," he thought sadly to himself.

His fishing rod was standing in the corner of his bedroom and his plane was sitting on top of his bookshelf. One by one, all his hopes about going to the coast were now crashing down around him in tatters.

"I'm going to have the worst weekend of my life," he said mournfully.

With that, he grabbed his sweater and went downstairs to join Granny. She was standing in the hallway dressed in her usual dark blue coat with a bright yellow scarf neatly tied around her neck.

The twins were eagerly sitting up in their buggy, laughing and smiling, safely buckled up ready for their walk to the park.

Sam just looked at them.

They didn't care about going to the coast.

How could they?

They were just BABIES!

Sam carefully held the gate open for his Granny to manoeuvre the buggy through. It was quite a large buggy and Sam felt a bit embarrassed being seen with it.

As they walked along the path towards the park, Sam winced as he saw his school friend Greg walking towards them.

"Hello," said Greg smirking, as he saw Sam. "I'm surprised to see you; I thought you were going away tonight."

Sam looked at him miserably, but before he had a chance to reply, his Granny started to explain.

"Unfortunately Sam's parents have been delayed at work, so at the moment he's unable to go until we see what happens."

"Oh, that's disappointing, but never mind, perhaps you can go next weekend instead. At least you'll have plenty of time now to finish your homework," said Greg.

Sam just glared back at him. He knew that secretly Greg was pleased about this. Sam was also thinking that next weekend was too far away. Besides, what if his parents had to work that weekend too?

Sam and Granny continued with their walk to the park in silence. There was a long queue for the ice cream and as they stood there waiting to be served Sam started to question his Granny again.

"Do you think you'll you be sleeping at our house tonight then Granny?"

"I expect so," she said.

"The twins will need feeding, bathing and putting to bed. So when I've done that perhaps you and I can have a little chat. Maybe look at your homework, or play a board game together before you go to bed."

"Would you like that?"

"Yes Granny. That would be great," replied Sam, trying his best to sound enthusiastic.

The ice cream man carefully handed Sam his cornet. "Here you go young man. You'd better eat it quickly before it melts," he said laughing. Sam quickly licked the edges of the ice cream to stop it running down his fingers.

His Granny pointed towards a nearby seat.

"Let's go and sit down over there on that seat. Then we can give Amy and Jessica some of our ice cream too."

Sam broke off the bottom of his cornet and scooped some ice-cream on it to give to Amy. Granny did the same for Jessica. Sam looked at his baby sisters and suddenly broke into fits of laughter. They had managed to get ice cream all around their faces and in between their fingers. They were laughing and giggling so much that it made Sam laugh too.

"What a mess they're making Granny. They'll certainly need a bath tonight," said Sam smiling.

"Yes they will, but at least they're having fun Sam," said Granny smiling. Sam looked at Amy and Jessica, they were only one year old and Sam couldn't wait for them to grow up so he could interact with them more.

Sam was ten years old and felt really excited when his Mum told him she was expecting twins. In fact he thought it was really special, having two babies at the same time. When the twins were born, Sam wasn't the slightest bit disappointed to have twin sisters instead of brothers.

To make the arrival of the twins even more special for Sam, his parents had bought him a second hand piano and guitar. From being quite young, Sam had shown a natural interest in music. When the piano arrived he found bundles of sheet music and a tutorial inside the piano stool, which gave him the motivation to want to learn more, so his parents arranged for him to have music lessons. Music and football were the two hobbies that Sam enjoyed the most.

As they walked home from the park, Sam asked Granny how long it would be before Amy and Jessica would be able to walk and talk?

"Well Sam, they're already beginning to crawl and they have a few teeth. But babies take time to do things. They need to learn how to feed themselves, and then they usually start to hold on to the furniture before they begin to let go and walk," she explained.

"Your Mum and Dad spent lots of time with you when you were a baby. They were always taking you out for walks to the park so that you could play on the swings and the roundabouts, and I can very clearly remember the day that you took your very first steps Sam," she said smiling.

"I can't remember doing any of that," said Sam.

"Oh yes Sam," she continued.

"Your parents took you to the park, the beach, the coast and many times to the funfair." But Sam had forgotten all about these things.

"So we used to have fun sometimes then?" he asked curiously.

"Of course you did Sam. Your Mum and Dad love you very much," answered his Granny. Feeling a bit happier, Sam sat for a few more minutes watching the birds pecking at crumbs from the ground.

"Have you finished your cornet Sam? It's time we were heading back home now," said Granny. Sam wiped his hands down the sides of his trousers and smiled at her. He took hold of the buggy and released the brake.

"Thank you for the ice cream. I'll push the buggy for you Granny, and when we get home, would you like me to help you get the twins ready for bed?"

"Yes that would be a great help Sam," she said ruffling his hair affectionately.

When they got back home, Sam began to get the twins clothes ready for bath time. He picked out clean nightwear and bibs from the drawers and then watched patiently as Granny bathed, fed and took Amy and Jessica in turn to their nursery.

Luckily the twins settled straight to sleep, so Granny was able to go back into the kitchen to tidy away their dirty dishes and prepare supper for her and Sam.

"Now then, what would you like to eat Sam?" said Granny.

Sam looked at her glumly. By now they would have all been at the coast tucking into fish and chips watching the waves roll in from the sea.

"I'm not so hungry, can I just have some cheese on toast please?"

"Of course you can. In the meantime, be a good lad and set the table for me please."

As his Granny was busy preparing supper, Sam watched and thought that perhaps it wasn't too bad having her stay. But it would have been a lot more fun if his Mum and Dad had taken them all to the coast.

2
Man of the Match

Sam loved going to the cottage. The holiday complex included a massive football field, a swimming pool and a tennis court. But he also enjoyed going to the coast because he was mesmerised by the sound of the sea.

Gathering sea shells was one of Sam's hobbies and over the years he had quite a collection of them sitting on his bedroom window sill. He loved to watch the waves as they came rolling in and sometimes his Dad took him body boarding too. He got really excited when he caught a wave and it carried him back onto the beach.

These were the things that Sam was so much looking forward to, but now his plans had been turned upside down.

As Sam and his Granny sat down to eat supper together, she could see that Sam was still feeling a bit despondent, so she tried to cheer him up by telling him a joke.

"What do you call a one eyed Dinosaur Sam?" "I don't know Granny," answered Sam smiling.

"*Do – u – think – he – saw - us,*" replied Granny laughing.

"Oh Granny, that's so funny. I'll have to remember to tell that one to Greg on Monday," he said.

Secretly, Sam thought his Granny was really funny. Some of the jokes she told him were hilarious because sometimes she used to forget the endings, which made him laugh even more.

"When I've finished supper, can I play football outside in the garden please?"

"Of course you can. I'll call you in before it gets too dark," she replied smiling.

Sam quickly finished his supper and went to get his football out from the garage.

"Oh that's good," he said as he picked the ball up and pressed it hard with his fingers. "It hasn't deflated, it's definitely hard enough to kick." The back garden was quite large and Sam's Dad had set up some miniature goal posts for him, along with a variety of swings and playthings for the twins. Sam would often pretend he was playing football for a world famous team.

He would imagine the crowd calling out his name and cheering him on! Although he was happy enough playing alone, he loved it even more when his Dad came into the garden to play football with him too.

Sam had been kicking the ball around for quite some time. It was gradually getting dark and the game was drawing to a close, but his 'imaginary' team were losing 2-1.

How could they manage to score a winning goal in such a short space of time?

Sam summoned up all the determination he could find, and carefully dribbled the ball across the garden.

Confidently weaving it from left to right, his nimble feet were swiftly dancing all over the grass. Just as the ball was about to go 'off-side' Sam rescued it just in time, then with a mighty kick ~ WHAM ~ it was safely landed in the back of the net! Sam lifted up his arms and punched the air with his fists in triumph.

Now he only had one more goal to score and his team had won the match. Once again he dribbled the ball with expert ease. Round and round he twisted and turned and with careful aim at the goal posts, he squared up to the centre of the net and WHAM!

Straight into the back of the net again!

Sam turned to the 'crowd,' who were by now giving him a standing ovation. The cheers went up. Sam Green had done it again! The team were saved from relegation and Sam was *'Man of the Match'*. Sam's cheeks were burning with all the running and excitement, but it would have been even more perfect, if his Dad had been there to witness him scoring the goals.

"Sam ~ Sam, It's time to come in now. It's getting dark."

"Coming Granny," he shouted, as he looked down at his jeans. They were really dirty from the grass stains, and somehow he had managed to tear a hole in both knees! Now Granny would have to mend his jeans and his school bag too!

Sam walked into the kitchen and hearing his footsteps Granny turned around from the kitchen sink.

"My goodness me," she said, shocked at seeing the state of him.

"What a mess you've made of your jeans, and look at the big holes you've put in them. Why don't you put these dirty clothes into the laundry basket and have your bath?"

"By the way Sam, what happened to your school bag? I've noticed it's ripped at the side."

"Oh I'm sorry Granny, I trapped it in the gate when I was coming home tonight. I was rushing home to see Mum and Dad and didn't see the nail sticking out at the side of the gate. Dad will need to get his toolbox out and mend the gate when he can."

"Never mind, I'll sew your bag for you tonight, and I'll mend your trousers too; it will give me something to do while I wait for your Mum and Dad to arrive."

"Now off you go. Don't worry you won't even notice they've been torn when I've finished with them."

Sam went upstairs to the bathroom to fill the tub. He waited patiently for the water to cool down and then stepped into the bath. As he began bathing himself, he looked down at his small legs and his thoughts began to wander. "Someday, these legs are going to be big and strong and I'm going to play football for a real team," he said to himself.

Sam began to wash his face and neck and as he splashed the water over his shoulders, he thought back to the football game he had just played in the back garden, and how great it felt to score the two winning goals.

He had been sitting so long day dreaming in the bath, that his fingers had begun to 'prune' and the water was now very cold.

Quickly stepping out of the bath he began to dry himself thoroughly. He cleaned his teeth, put on his pyjamas and his favourite bright red dressing gown, then went downstairs to say goodnight to Granny.

"I'm ready for bed now Granny. I've had my bath, brushed my teeth and put my clothes in the laundry basket as you asked."

His Granny looked at him and gave him a big hug.

"You know Sam, your parents are really proud of you, and I know they'll be very sorry about this weekend. But look how much fun you've had going to the park for the ice cream and playing football in the garden."

"Come on now, I'll make you a nice mug of hot chocolate and then we'll have a chat about your homework."

Sam loved the hot chocolate Granny made him because she sprinkled tiny vanilla marshmallows on top. When he had finished his drink, Sam put his mug in the dishwasher and had a look through the geography homework he'd been given.

"Oh it's not hard at all Granny; I'll be able to do that first thing in the morning," he said.

"Well, what about playing that board game now Sam?" asked Granny.

"OK, I bet you get more points than I do," he said laughing.

Sam and Granny spent the next half an hour playing the game, until Sam could feel his eyes getting tired.

"I think I need to go to bed now," he said yawning. "Mum and Dad haven't phoned, so I guess I'll see them in the morning."

"OK, off you go. I'll be up in a minute to tuck you in," said Granny.

Even though Sam didn't feel it necessary for her to do that, he didn't mind because he knew that she loved him.

Sam then quietly tip-toed upstairs to his bedroom; the twins were fast asleep in their nursery and as Sam passed the nursery door, he peeped in to look at them before going into his own bedroom. They looked so adorable, that he wondered if he had looked like that too when he was a baby. Sam's Granny had followed him upstairs and was now standing behind him. She gently tapped him on the shoulder.

"Come along Sam, let's get you into bed."

Sam took off his dressing gown and slippers and climbed into his cosy bed. He pulled the duvet tight up to his chin. It was a very special duvet, with pictures of footballs all over it. Sam's bedroom was a football haven. His bedroom walls were covered in pictures of famous players and he had a football shaped light shade hanging from his ceiling. A personally signed football shirt from his favourite team took pride of place on his bedroom wall, and he even had a signed football from them too, which always sat proudly by his bedside. Sam never kicked that particular ball around because it was just too special to use!

"One day Granny, I'm going to be a famous football player," he said, *as she turned off his bedroom light.*

"Yes I can believe that Sam," said Granny gently stroking the top of his head.

Sam smiled at her and snuggled down into his cosy bed, then pulling his duvet up to his chin he closed his eyes.

3

A Fantastic Opportunity

Soon Sam was fast asleep and dreaming.

"Come on Sam, we need you to be the Captain of the Team today. Greg's Mum has rang in to say that he's had an accident and broken his arm."

Sam was astonished.

"Come on Sam, hurry up. Everyone's waiting," urged Mr. Harrison his PE Teacher.

"But I don't think I'm the best player. I think you ought to ask Henry. He's a far better player than I am."

Just then a little voice interrupted the conversation.

"Don't turn this opportunity down Sam. It's what you've been waiting for."

Sam immediately looked around to see where the voice was coming from. He was absolutely flabbergasted to see a small talking bear standing in front of him.

He was wearing a full football strip complete with boots. He also had Sam's treasured football tucked underneath his arm.

"Who are you?" asked Sam curiously.

"I'm Dodl, and I'm here to show you what a wonderful future is waiting for you, when you take the opportunities that are going to present themselves to you."

"I know you have a dream Sam to become a world famous football player, but that dream won't become your reality if you continue to turn down chances when they appear," declared Dodl.

Sam looked at the bear and then around at all his friends, but remarkably his friends and Mr Harrison had now disappeared!

They were nowhere to be seen.

He was now standing alone with only the talking bear for company.

"Where am I? Where have all my friends gone and how do you know my name?" Sam asked curiously.

"Oh dear me Sam, I know all about you. I know that you are ten years old and you have twin sisters whose names are Jessica and Amy. I also know that you enjoy playing football and playing the guitar and piano. You see I know all about you."

"You are now standing in The Field of Dreams in a place called The Magical World of Fingley, and when you get to know me a little bit better, you will understand more about my role and what my purpose is."

"My name Dodl means Doing Ordinary Deeds Lovingly, so I have interrupted your dream tonight to make your acquaintance, and show you the wonderful future that's waiting for you."

Sam was getting more curious by the minute.

"But in order for you to take advantage of my visit, you must place your trust in me to have the knowledge and the ability to take you into the *future*."

"You will no doubt have observed that I have special *purple paws* and feet. You may think this strange, but there is a perfectly good explanation. In order for me to enter into dreams I also needed to be able to travel into the *future* and into the *past*."

"I have a wonderful companion, who you will be able to meet later named Orb. He is a Wizard Bear, and it was he who enabled me to receive the ability to travel through time."

"He did this by asking me to hold a magical amethyst crystal and repeat some magic words. So you can now see with your own eyes that this has happened. It was an opportunity presented to me that I accepted without hesitation."

"Over time, Orb and I have visited many young people and adults too inviting them to The Magical World of Fingley to have amazing adventures."

"It is also *my purpose* to write about these adventures, so the stories will never be lost, but will serve as an inspiration to children just like you."

Sam was speechless.

Here he was, standing in a massive field, talking with a bear named Dodl, who had purple paws and feet explaining that he could Time Travel!

Sam laughed and laughed.

"Oh Dodl that's the best laugh I've had in ages. You can't possibly be real. This is only a dream ~ isn't it?"

"It may only be a dream to you Sam, but it's perfectly real to me. But let me now ask you a question."

"Would you like to play in the World Cup, and become a real 'Man of the Match'?"

"Oh yes Dodl, I would," replied Sam.

Very well then, we have no time to lose. Quickly take my paw and keep tight hold of it, because you're in for the journey of a lifetime. But before we begin, you must promise me that you'll remember this adventure for the rest of your life."

"Oh of course, yes. I promise Dodl," said Sam enthusiastically.

"Very well Sam, take my paw and close your eyes."

Sam did as Dodl asked. He closed his eyes and held on to Dodl's paw as tightly as he could. Suddenly Sam could feel the wind blowing through his hair and the summer sun warming his fingers as he held on to Dodl's paw. He felt as though he was travelling through a tunnel.

They were spinning round and round. Up and down, over and over. Sam was beginning to feel rather dizzy.

"Keep your eyes closed Sam, we're nearly there," called out Dodl.

"Not long now!" No sooner were Dodl's words said than they both landed firmly on the ground.

"You can open your eyes now Sam," whispered Dodl.

Sam felt his feet land on the ground. He was still holding tightly on to Dodl's paw and couldn't wait to open his eyes. As he blinked, he was astounded to see the biggest football stadium of his life.

It was enormous, and there were thousands of people seated all around it.

"Where am I," he uttered.

As Sam looked around, he also saw that Dodl was now much smaller than when he first met him. But this was because Sam was now much taller ... and much OLDER!

Sam looked down expecting to see his small skinny legs but he was completely and utterly staggered to see that he was now fully grown!

"Come along Sam. The changing rooms are over there," said Dodl pointing to the back of the stadium.

"You'll need to get changed quickly; the team are waiting for you."

"But ... but." "No BUT'S Sam."

"Quickly, go and get changed," snapped Dodl.

Sam ran towards the arena and found the changing rooms. Remarkably the team of players were all waiting for him.

"Come on Sam, hurry up, time is passing and the Ref will be waiting for us," said one of the players. Sam looked at the player speaking to him and followed him to the changing rooms. He didn't recognise him at all, but quickly changed into the football strip that was hanging from the rail.

The whole team then assembled, and as he lined up with them all, Sam could hear the crowd shouting his name.

"Sam Green, Sam Green."

He couldn't believe what he was hearing.

He looked at the other players.

They were all smiling at him, and jumping up and down to warm up ready for the game.

They finally received the signal to walk onto the pitch with their mascot. Sam stared in disbelief.

The mascot was a young blond haired boy who looked just like him!

4

The Adventure of a Life-Time

It was late that night when Sam's parents finally arrived home from work and Granny was sitting in the lounge quietly reading her newspaper.

"Hello Mum, we're sorry to be so late," said Sam's Mum, interrupting the silence.

"Are the children alright?" she asked, as she quickly took off her coat.

"They're fine," Granny replied.

"Although Sam was a bit upset when he realised you were both at work and you wouldn't be able to go to the coast tonight."

"I thought he would be," interrupted Sam's Dad.

"I feel terrible about making that promise and then having to break it, but never mind, perhaps we can arrange something else to make it up to him."

Sam's Dad looked thoughtful. "I hope he understands. I know he really wants me to take him to the football match next week because his favourite team are playing at home, but I'm not sure at the moment if I can."

"Oh Ben, I do hope you will, because he'll be very disappointed to miss that too," said Granny.

"But it's getting late. I've made some supper for you both in the kitchen. I'll go and get it ready for you."

Sam's parents sat around the kitchen table quietly eating their supper, when Granny came into the kitchen to say goodnight.

"I've been thinking, Molly. I'd be happy to stay for a few days, if that would help?"

"Oh thank you. That would be great Mum, shall we talk about it in the morning?"

"Thank you for making a meal for us too," said Molly putting the dishes into the kitchen sink. "You must be tired Mum I think we all need to go to bed now. See you in the morning," said Molly.

"OK Molly, goodnight, leave the dishes and get off to bed. I can turn off the lights and tidy things up here," said Granny.

Molly and Ben quietly climbed the stairs so as not to waken the twins and Sam. They peered into the twin's nursery and then into Sam's bedroom. Sam was fast asleep.

He was holding tightly onto his football. Molly carefully moved it from out of his arms, and gently pulled his duvet over his shoulders.

Then they both walked quietly into their own bedroom, and as Molly sat on the edge of their bed, she let out a deep sigh!

"You know Ben, I wish we didn't have to work such long hours. We can't really expect Sam to understand why we both need to be at work. I do hope he's not too upset."

Sam wasn't really old enough to fully understand the reason his parents had to give so much time to work, but it was because they owned their own company that made roof tiles.

They had factories in different locations and employed over a hundred people, so it was quite a big responsibility. As Sam grew older, Ben had occasionally taken him around one of the factories to explain how the roof tiles were made. He showed him how the newly made tiles were gently dried in the 'curing chamber' before being burnt in the kiln. Ben was hoping that one day Sam would work in the company too, but for now, all he wanted was a good night's sleep.

Molly knew that Ben also felt disappointed at not being able to go to the cottage. She sat at the side of him and put her arms around him.

"I know you feel upset about Sam and the weekend as much as I do, but I also worry about the twins."

"Mum is really helpful, but I feel I'm missing so much of their precious early years," said Molly.

"I really would like to spend more time with them. Although I work flexi-time when you need me, surely we can find a way to have weekends free and make more of an effort to go to the coast?"

"Sam does need time and attention, and he was so looking forward to going to the cottage today," she said sighing.

"Let's talk about it all in the morning Molly. Right now, we both need to get some sleep," said Ben wearily.

Molly and Ben settled into their bed. Turned off their bedside lights and in no time at all, they were both fast asleep.

Then suddenly, a voice sounded …

"It's a goal! Sam Green has scored in the last minute of The World Cup."

Molly and Ben were so startled they shot bolt upright in bed. Looking around their bedroom, they saw what appeared to be a small talking bear. He was standing on the dressing table stool, looking intently at both of them.

He was holding a football in one paw and waving a football rattle in the other, which was making the most incredibly loud noise.

"HELLO I'M DODL."

"I do apologise for the extremely loud noise because I know how terribly tired you both are," exclaimed the talking bear.

"I expect you're both wondering why I'm disturbing your sleep at such a late hour."

Molly and Ben looked in amazement at each other. Molly rubbed her eyes.

"I think I'm dreaming," she said, looking sleepily at Ben.

Ben looked down at the extraordinary bear and then at Molly, as Dodl continued to speak.

"Please let me introduce myself to you," Dodl continued.

"As I just told you, my name is Dodl and I know immediately what you must be thinking. You must be wondering why I have arrived here in your bedroom, at this extremely late hour. Well, I have been observing you and your family for quite some time, and feel that this very moment would be most appropriate to make my visit."

Molly and Ben stared in disbelief at the scene before them. Dodl spoke solemnly:

"The children of our world are precious, as you are both well aware."

"They need *all* kinds of care."

"But one of the most precious kinds of care is *HAVING FUN.*" Dodl then continued:

"Parents and guardians are so busy these days working long hours to provide for their family, that at times they've forgotten how to have fun. So my role is to come along at exactly the right moment to deliver this little reminder."

"So with that in mind, before we go any further, I would like to ask whether *you* are both ready to begin the adventure of a life-time and to have some *FUN* yourselves?"

Molly and Ben looked inquisitively at each other.

"Well, I'm not quite sure what you mean, but yes, I suppose we are," said Ben curiously.

"Very good," continued Dodl.

"Please meet me downstairs in the front garden where I will introduce you to my most trusted and valued companion. His name is Aura. He is a magnificent creature and one that I'm sure you will be fascinated to meet."

Dodl immediately jumped down from the dressing table stool and disappeared into thin air.

"Well, what do you make of that?" said Molly as she grabbed her dressing gown from the back of the bedroom door.

"Here Ben, put on your dressing gown and take your scarf. You'll need it to keep you warm if we're going to be outside for a while."

Molly and Ben didn't know what to expect as they quickly put on their dressing gowns and slippers. They quietly tip-toed downstairs and opened the front door.

"Oh my goodness," shrieked Molly.

They were immediately greeted by the surprise of their life. There standing before them bathed in the light of the full moon was the most magnificent creature either of them had ever seen.

They instantly recognised the horn of a Unicorn, but it also had the golden tipped wings of Pegasus too. It was happily munching away at the grass in their garden.

Proudly seated on its back was the same little bear that had interrupted their sleep.

"Quickly, time is precious. Do please join me," said Dodl waving his arms around.

As he spoke, the magical creature lifted its head from the grass. He looked intently at Molly and Ben and then gently bent first one knee, then the other, so they could both climb on his back.

"This is Aura; he is my most trusted and loyal friend. You will of course recognise the magical horn of the Unicorn, but also the wings of Pegasus that enable him to fly!"

"Aura is here to take you on the most incredible and magical adventure that you have ever experienced."

"Hello Dodl," said Ben, feeling a little bit strange addressing a talking bear!

"Molly and I are very pleased to meet you both, but we are really curious as to how you managed to appear in our bedroom, and also *where* exactly do you intend to take us?"

"All will be revealed in the fullness of time and then you will realise the intention of my visit," replied Dodl as he grasped hold of Aura's silver mane with his paw.

"For now, climb up, hold tight and prepare for the journey of a lifetime!"

5

The Aurora Borealis

Ben climbed high up onto Aura, and held out his hand to help pull Molly up. As soon as all three of them were safely sitting on Aura's back, Aura lifted his head and began to strike the ground with his golden hoof.

Then right there on the spot, he began to quickly 'spin' around and around.

"Hold tight Molly," shouted Ben anxiously.

Both Molly and Ben quickly felt dizzy. They became even dizzier the faster that Aura twirled. Suddenly, from out of the darkness of the night sky came millions of twinkling bright stars. They were burning so brightly, that even Dodl had to hide his eyes with his paws.

"Please hold on tightly, because what you're both about to experience is the most magnificent splendour that nature can provide."

No sooner had Dodl spoken, than the dark night sky suddenly began to change colour. Majestic swathes of bright green, vivid gold and purple stretched for miles before them, providing a ribbon-like canopy.

The colours were moving and shifting as if on a giant canvas. Aura powered onwards through them. His long silvery mane and tail were billowing out behind him. His golden tipped wings extended to their full span as the colours shifted and changed, glowing even brighter.

Ben and Molly were both holding on tightly, exhilarated by all they were seeing. Never before had they witnessed such a beautiful and extensive sight.

They were travelling at the speed of light!

"Isn't this amazing?" shouted Dodl.

The colours were electrifying!

Molly held on tightly to Ben and Aura as they continued to gallop through the never-ending spectacle. But then, just as quickly as the stars and colours had appeared, the night sky began to change. Aura was climbing higher and higher now. His powerful legs were pushing through the atmosphere. The colours seemed to be underneath them now as they began to cross over continents.

Flames of colour were filling the sky. The dancing lights and streamers were intermittently blending with curtains of shooting rays of colour.

The sky was alight with an incredible glow. Molly could clearly see the oceans flowing beneath them. Mountain ranges appeared and then disappeared.

Ben and Molly were gasping with delight. They both felt as if they were flying across the World!

"If only Sam could see this," shouted Ben.

As the night sky gradually reappeared, Aura slowed his pace. His body heaving and panting with exertion. As he did so, the darkness began to fade and lighten. The daylight was breaking and the birds were welcoming the day with their dawn chorus. Aura gracefully landed into a 'trot' on the green grass beneath his hooves. Dodl began speaking once more.

"My dear friends, you have just witnessed the magnificent Aurora Borealis, most commonly referred to as the Northern Lights. However, because we have travelled through time from the Northern Hemisphere to the Southern Hemisphere, you have also witnessed the Aurora Australis too. Hence my friends, you have travelled across the world!"

After making this astonishing declaration, Dodl continued, his words were full of excitement.

"These incredible lights are usually seen after dusk near both Poles. This phenomenon was named after Aurora the Roman Goddess of the Dawn, and the Greek name for the wind is Boreas; facts that your son Sam is probably aware of because of his immense interest in geography."

"Although they look elegant and calm, aurorae are produced from millions of explosions of magnetic energy. I am aware of this you see, because during my travels I have lived amongst the stars and witnessed this amazing spectacle many, many times before."

Molly and Ben were overwhelmed and speechless as they both held on tightly to Aura's mane.

They were still reeling from the experience of the amazing colours and the excitement of the ride. Dodl could see they were not only impressed with his eloquent explanation, but trembling with excitement from the adventure too!

He realised they were both finding the events completely breath-taking, as he continued to explain.

"Do you see, and more importantly, have you felt, enjoyed, and learned so much from this fun experience?" asked Dodl.

"Perhaps you might like to dismount and sit for a while there," he said, pointing to a patch of grass.

Ben helped Molly down from Aura's back and as they looked around them, they could see the dawn light twinkling through the trees; their curiosity was increasing with each moment.

"Where are we now?" asked Molly.

"You are now in The Magical World of Fingley. This is where you will meet some of my extraordinary friends," replied Dodl.

"All will be revealed in due course. But first I need to lead you through the Hazel and Oak Wood and onwards to Cobblestones."

Dodl took hold of Aura's long silvery mane and began to gently guide him through the Hazel and Oak Wood. Ozzy the owl suddenly flew overhead. As Guardian of the Hazel and Oak Wood, he automatically knew when visitors had arrived, and his responsibility was to see them all safely through the woods and onto The Field of

Dreams. Molly was gripping Ben's hand tightly as they walked slowly through the woods. The woodland creatures were stirring and the birds were welcoming the dawn with their chorus.

Slowly, as the path began to wind round to the right, Dodl stretched out his paw and pointed to the huge piece of open space before them.

"This is The Field of Dreams," he said with great delight.

6

The Magical World of Fingley

Molly and Ben looked around them. They were intrigued to see lots of different styles of houses and buildings. Some were built in tiny clusters and some were standing tall and proud.

"Oh Ben! Who do you think could possibly live in a place like this? I've never seen houses like this before. They're absolutely incredible," whispered Molly.

Dodl tugged on Aura's mane and commanded him to stand still. Turning proudly to Molly and Ben, he then began to tell the next part of his story.

"I arrived in your bedroom this evening with a very specific task. That task was to bring you to The Magical World of Fingley to visit my home Cobblestones, and to introduce you to some of my very special friends. I am doing this to help you understand a little more about yourselves and also your precious children, Sam, Amy and Jessica."

He then continued:

"You see my friends, sometimes we Fingley Folk feel that parents are so busy working to provide for their families; they forget they too need to have fun."

"Please, come with me a little bit further. I would like to introduce you to my friend Orb. He is the most amazing wizard bear you will ever meet. I know that he would like to tell you something that perhaps you might not be fully aware of."

Holding each other's hand tightly, Molly and Ben walked directly behind Dodl as he led them onto a garden path. This took them straight to the front door of Cobblestones. As they were about to knock on the door it immediately opened, as though someone was expecting them. Molly and Ben stood in amazement, both of them gazing at the sight before them.

"Hello, my name is Amber. I'm very pleased to meet you. Welcome to The Magical World of Fingley and our home Cobblestones."

Amber held out her hand in welcome. Molly smiled and stepped forward to shake Amber's dainty hand then stepped aside to let Ben do the same.

Amber was dressed in a dazzling emerald green dress and wore an Amber necklace around her tiny neck. Her wings were gossamer thin, and her honey coloured hair fell in long, tumbling curls around her shoulders. Molly and Ben looked in amazement at the vision before them. They knew it was real, because they were experiencing it. But so many questions were buzzing around their heads.

Who? What? Why? Where? How?

Without further ado, Dodl stepped forward to greet his friend.

"Hello Amber, I'm sorry it's taken me so long to get here, but we had a slight detour along the way, which I'll tell you about later."

"Don't worry about that Dodl, you're here now, so please do come in," said Amber leading the way.

Cobblestones was a very interesting house and Molly couldn't wait to see more of it. From the hallway, a large wood panelled door led them into a sizeable area that contained a fireplace, upon which hung a sign inscribed with the words:

'Expect a Miracle'

Dodl caught sight of Molly reading the sign. "Yes, that's a most interesting sign indeed, don't you agree?" asked Dodl.

Molly nodded her head and gasped as she saw the most amazing wooden staircase.

It was intricately carved and the steps seemed to go on forever. Molly also noticed that it featured the outline of a strange and mysterious face that had been carved into it.

She was just about to ask Dodl about it when he interrupted Molly's thoughts by pointing to the small cupboard door underneath the stairs.

"Soon, you'll understand even more, but in the meantime, I'd like to introduce you to a few more of my friends."

No sooner had the words left Dodl's lips than the small door under the stairs began to slowly open.

"May I introduce you to four of my very special friends?"

Immediately from out the cupboard under the stairs, walked three curious small bears, followed by a much larger and older bear who was wearing spectacles.

They were all smiling at Molly and Ben as if they were expecting them.

"These are my friends!" exclaimed Dodl.

"This is Expect a Miracle, Soul Mates, Earth Angel and last, but certainly not least, Orb the Wizard Bear."

The three bears were all wearing t-shirts with their names written on the front. They held out their paws in a warm and welcoming gesture. Orb then stepped forward and shook hands firmly with both Molly and Ben.

"Welcome to Cobblestones," he said warmly. His kind voice gently streamed out like warm honey.

"Please, take a seat," he said, gesturing towards a rather old but comfortable looking sofa. It stood against the wall overlooking a beautifully kept garden. Molly and Ben sat silently side by side, eagerly waiting to hear more.

"Well first of all, let me welcome you to The Magical World of Fingley," continued Orb.

"I understand from my friend Dodl, that you are the parents of three wonderful children named Sam, Amy and Jessica."

"He also tells me that over the past few years, you have found yourselves more and more absorbed and involved in your work, thereby finding it quite difficult to step aside from this to take time out to HAVE FUN!"

Orb popped his spectacles to the end of his nose and peered through them intently at Molly and Ben. After studying them both for a few seconds, he continued:

"I feel that the time has now arrived to bring to your attention the serious situation that has arisen right under your noses so to speak, without you being aware of it."

"When Sam was born, you were both overjoyed with his arrival. You took him to the park, the playground, the coast and the zoo. You spent lots of time with him, and you enjoyed watching him giggle and laugh, as you Ben flew his kite with him."

"He grew up for several years quite alone without brothers or sisters. But then along came Amy and Jessica, twin little girls who quite understandably took attention away from Sam for a time."

"However, Sam never showed any resentment. In fact he was immensely happy to have such special little girls as his sisters and accepted the situation quite happily."

"I also realise that the arrival of two little girls at the same time, brought extra responsibilities financially, and caring for them both was time consuming. In fact it has not been an easy time for any of you."

"However, this cannot be used as an excuse for not spending valuable time now with Sam."

"He needs your time as well as your love."

"He needs his sisters and his Granny too. In buying the cottage, you found a solution for all of you to be able to spend time together having fun."

Orb looked thoughtfully at Ben and Molly.

"I have already spoken to you about how readily Sam accepted the arrival of his two little sisters, never once complaining that he would have liked a brother. Sam is an amazing young boy. He is intelligent, gentle, kind and caring. He looks up to you Ben and eagerly awaits your homecoming so that you can both spend time together playing football in your garden."

"With all this in mind and in order for you to completely understand, I would like to invite you both on another adventure with Aura."

"So please prepare to embark upon a new journey, and a new understanding that will change your lives forever."

Molly and Ben looked thoughtfully at each other. They both felt as though they had been summoned to the Headmaster's room!

But it was true; they had gradually over the years found themselves in a rut. The promises they had made to Sam at various times were often broken. But Sam had always been a kind and caring boy.

He never *seemed* to have got too upset by this.

But now Orb had told them that Sam had kept all this sadness to himself, not wanting to upset his parents.

What could they do to make things better?

Soon they were about to find out!

The Future is Waiting

After listening to Orb speak, Dodl began to explain to Molly and Ben what he proposed they do next.

"Orb has very kindly put you in the picture, now it's time for you to make a very special journey. We are able to travel into the *future* with the aid of Orb's Time-Travelling Tunnel, to give yourselves a glimpse of the life that awaits Sam."

"Please follow me outside. We will ride on Aura again, but also with Orb this time."

Molly and Ben glanced at each other. How on earth was all this going to happen?

How could they be transported into the future?

Events were getting more curious with each passing moment. However, they dutifully followed Dodl and Orb into the garden. There before them once again, stood Aura. He was patiently waiting for them all to join him. The beautiful Pegacorn knelt before them all.

Orb stepped up first, followed closely by Dodl. Then Ben climbed up and held his hand out to pull Molly up too. Once everyone was settled on Aura's strong sturdy back, Orb gently tugged at Aura's flowing mane.

"Forward Aura," he commanded.

"IT IS TIME TO FLY!"

Upon Orb's command, Aura began to gallop across The Field of Dreams. Gradually his golden tipped hooves left the ground and they were instantly airborne, as smoothly as a jet plane reaching for the skies. Up and up they went, past the houses far below. Aura gained height with every movement of his body.

His enormous golden tipped wings were pushing through the air, leaving The Field of Dreams far below them. Suddenly the whole world seemed to be spinning. Colours of every hue were dancing all around them.

"Hold on tight everyone," called Dodl.

"The future is waiting for us."

Without warning, mystical music flowed all around them and indescribable colours of every hue were spinning and dancing in front of their eyes. Molly and Ben both felt as though they were being pulled into a new and strange dimension!

Molly had her arms gripped tightly around Ben's waist and Dodl held tight onto Aura's glistening mane as they all went rushing into the next part of this thrilling adventure.

Far below them were rivers and fields and after what seemed forever, Aura began to slow his speed. Molly felt her stomach lurch and whirl.

She remembered this was the same feeling she used to feel on the Big Dipper or the Big

Wheel when she went to the fairground as a young girl. It was a sensation that she hadn't felt since then, but now her memories came flooding back.

Molly remembered all the times that she *HAD FUN* in her childhood.

She remembered how her parents had taken her to play in the ocean, and how much she enjoyed holding the sea shells to her ear so she could hear the sea rolling in. She thought about the times she had spent with her grandparents too. How she had watched her Granny bake bread and cakes for special treats for birthdays, and making jellies that looked like a rabbit when she 'plopped' them out of the jelly mould.

Ben also had his eyes closed. He too was remembering all the times he'd spent with his older brother Tim and his own Dad when they used to go fishing together, and to rugby and football matches.

While Molly and Ben were busily remembering their childhood, Aura had slowly and gracefully landed on the soft green earth below them. Ben and Molly slowly opened their eyes.

Where were they now?

With a gentle tug on his mane, Dodl motioned to Aura to kneel so they could all alight. Aura immediately obeyed and knelt on the grass. One by one they all climbed down from Aura's back. Molly was still feeling very dizzy and clung on to Ben's arm. She straightened her dressing gown and pulled her slipper back onto her foot.

"Thank you Aura my friend, that was most enjoyable. Most enjoyable indeed. Don't you agree?" said Orb.

Molly and Ben gently patted Aura and feeling more composed, Molly held Aura's head in her hands.

"Thank you Aura" she said quietly.

"I shall never forget you, or the adventure that you've given us," she said affectionately.

"Look!" Ben cried out interrupting them.

Molly turned to see that Ben was pointing to an enormous building in the distance.

"What's that?" he said.

"That... is the Olympic Stadium, where your son Sam is playing football. He is a valued member of the National Team."

"But Sam isn't old enough to play football for a team yet, and especially not here in the Olympic Stadium," replied Ben feeling completely and utterly stunned.

"Oh yes he is! *Sam is now 22 years of age and is a very talented and gifted young man.*"

"Not only is he a very gifted football player, he is also a talented musician who plays the guitar and piano proficiently," said Dodl proudly.

"What! How did all this happen?" exclaimed Molly.

Orb interrupted the conversation.

"Sam was born with the gift of *patience*. It has been patience that has taught him how to listen, learn and to always try and overcome obstacles."

"He was an only child until the arrival of his twin sisters. However, Sam never felt envious or upset about that because he enjoyed playing with them."

Orb continued; "Sam had patience to wait for his sisters to grow up, knowing that one day he would be able to talk with them and enjoy spending time with them."

"So much so, that Amy used to love to listen to Sam as he played the piano, or strum his guitar. This then led him to sit and practise when you and Ben were at work. He practically taught himself to play."

"What you will see today, is the culmination of all of your efforts with Sam."

"Not only *your* efforts, but his Granny's, sisters and his friends. But this has only happened by taking time out to understand, have patience and *HAVE FUN*."

"Now, let us proceed into the stadium. Please walk this way," said Orb gesturing with his paw for the others to follow.

Obediently Molly, Ben and Dodl all followed Orb through the enormous gates into the stadium.

It was huge. The emerald green pitch was encircled by thousands of seats. Each seat was occupied by a devoted football fan, all shouting the name of just one player.

"SAM GREEN ~ SAM GREEN."

Over and over they chanted his name. Football rattles were being spun around making the most incredible and deafening sound. It was so loud that Molly and Ben couldn't hear themselves think, let alone speak. They both looked at the fantastic spectacle before them. How could their small young son be part of this amazing happening?

The crowd gradually fell silent as the players ran onto the pitch. The silence however quickly ended as Sam's team appeared.

Once again the shout went out;

"SAM GREEN~SAM GREEN."

The referee blew his whistle to signal the start of the game and a stilled silence descended all around the stadium. The ball was instantly passed from one player to another. The blue team took the ball and a big *groan* went out! Then the red team regained the ball.

A young player with the number 9 on his shirt immediately took control of it. He dribbled it away from the opposition.

Carefully and skilfully he shot by the other team members. He knew exactly where he was heading ~ the goal posts. The player then skilfully eyed up the goal posts and dodging the opposition, lined himself up with the centre of the net.

With one almighty kick ~ WHAM!

The ball was safely planted into the back of the net!

"SAM GREEN ~ SAM GREEN"

The excited crowd shouted out Sam's name. But this was no time for complacency!

Sam had scored the first goal, but now the opposing team were vying to get revenge and immediately equalised with a goal themselves. The game had begun in earnest, and the ball was dizzy on the pitch. The red team took possession of the ball and manoeuvred it towards the goal posts. Suddenly a blue team player shot across and controlled the ball. The blue team's number 7 player dribbled the ball carefully, not allowing anyone in.

He had acquired the ball and he was not about to let it go.

The players began trying to intercept the ball, but the number 7 player was determined to get the ball into the back of the net.

WHAM! He had successfully landed the ball in the goal. Immediately the Referee blew the whistle for half-time!

A 'boo' went up from the crowd. Time was running out!

"SAM ~ SAM" shouted the fans excitedly. A huge 'Mexican Wave' began to ripple through the stands.

Each fan stood holding up a massive piece of card. It had just one name written on it;

'SAM GREEN'

The game recommenced. The second half was proving to be just as nail-biting. The game was into its final minutes and the score was still equal. Molly and Ben looked anxiously at each other. They had seen their only son score the first goal, now they both knew that Sam had to score the second goal to secure the match.

Ben grabbed hold of Molly's hand.

"I know he can do it Molly. I know he can do it," said Ben shaking. No sooner had the words left Ben's lips, when they both gasped as they saw Sam take control of the ball.

This was not going to be easy though!

The defenders were all out to stop him! They crowded around him. It seemed as if the whole team was making a 'human wall' to prevent Sam from moving. But they were no match for Sam.

He left them all gasping and standing as he dribbled and interacted with the ball as if it was part of him. He controlled his movements with expert ease. He passed the ball to his team-mate, who then passed it back. Back and forth they both played across the width and length of the field. Sam was like lightning, as he ran with the ball. The minutes were ticking away!

He now had the ball in his control and he wasn't going to let it go at any price. He ran and ran, eyeing up the goal posts. He was now within shooting distance of the goal.

With what seemed like the speed of light, Sam squared up to the net and with one enormous kick, he landed the ball majestically into the back of it.

The referee blew his whistle. It was all over!
SAM HAD SECURED THE CUP!!
The crowd went WILD!

They stood and roared their approval. Ben and Molly stood up to applaud too. They were jumping up and down with excitement.

"He did it! He did it! Sam did it!" shouted Molly with tears running down her cheeks.

Molly and Ben hugged each other. The crowd were chanting Sam's name over and over. The players all took off their shirts and exchanged them. Sam was being lifted high into the air by his fellow players. He had a massive grin on his face. His team-mates carried him around the field in a lap of honour, the crowd still cheering and shouting his name.

Sam was such a young player, yet everyone knew he had a fantastic future ahead of him. The Team Manager came running onto the pitch to congratulate the players, especially Sam.

He had shown what a fantastic footballer he was, and what a tremendous achievement he had secured for his country, his team, his family and for himself.

8

Orb's Amazing Time-Tunnel

The crowd were still chanting Sam's name as they all began to disperse. Orb signalled to Molly and Ben to stay in their seats until everyone had left.

Slowly, the stadium cleared of people and Orb began to speak.

"You have now seen the bright and amazing future that is waiting for Sam."

"This potential is within him now. However, he will only achieve this dream if both of you realise and understand, that with each day, week, month and year that Sam grows, he is relying on your love and your time."

"He will only be able to harness this future if he spends quality time with his family, who can nurture and encourage him."

"Time spent *HAVING FUN* can be a time to learn, as I feel this has been proven to you both this very evening with your adventure to the Northern and Southern Hemispheres on Aura."

Orb continued. "Both of you have also witnessed how patience, understanding, kindness and encouragement; can be gained by *HAVING FUN*."

"Education can be an adventure!"

"Life does not have to be so serious. Life is precious. Time is precious, and your children will not remain children forever. So my dear friends, we have now shown you the potential future for your son Sam."

"However, he will not secure this alone. You must fulfil your roles too."

Dodl bear could not contain himself and felt compelled to show his appreciation.

"That's amazing Orb, you have spoken so profoundly. Thank you for your time and your wisdom."

Molly and Ben looked intently at each other. It was a pure 'A-ha' moment. The penny had dropped. In an instant, they both understood what needed to be done; their lives needed a new direction and a new purpose. *Work needed to be more balanced with HAVING FUN!* Dodl appeared anxious and interrupted the silence.

"Quickly! Quickly! We must hurry. We must meet with Aura once again to take us to our final destination."

All four of them quickly made their way out of the stadium and into the open space. There before them stood Aura. Once again they all sat up tall on Aura's back and without hesitation, the Pegacorn began to use his tremendous wings to lift them all high into the air. He instantly blended with the sky. Faster and faster he flew. The morning dawn gradually began to fade and the night-time stars appeared. Then one by one the stars too faded away, and morning soon became afternoon.

"Look beneath you," shouted Dodl.

As they did so, Molly and Ben could see Sam's school.

They could also see Sam running out of the school gate, across the playing field and down the street into their house. Suddenly, Molly and Ben realised what Dodl and Orb were doing.

They were taking them back, to yesterday!

Back to the *past*, so that they could see just how disappointed Sam had been, and yet how understanding he became when his Granny told him they were unable to go to the cottage. They watched as he sat in the park eating his ice cream. They watched him as he played football alone in his garden and saw the elation he felt as he scored the goal, wishing that his Dad could have seen him.

They watched as he sat with Granny when she looked at his homework with him. They watched everything, exactly as it had happened the previous day.

And they watched themselves too ~ at work! They saw that if they had tried harder to organise their time, they could have taken the family to the cottage.

"Do you see now, how fortunate you are to have such a special son as Sam? It is only with the wisdom and magic of Orb and his Time Tunnel, and the existence of The Magical World of Fingley and all who live there that we've been able to assess your situation and help you," said Dodl.

Aura continued to gallop onwards. The wind was blowing through Molly's hair and now she could see the houses below her. It was the street where they lived. Molly could clearly see the car in the driveway.

It was still dark. Aura began to slow down until his hooves finally met with the ground beneath them. Breathing heavily, he cantered to a final stop at the family home. Aura gently knelt on the grass in the front garden, allowing Molly, Ben, Dodl and Orb to once again dismount.

Dodl turned to Ben and Molly and began to speak.

"This very evening you have witnessed and experienced an amazing adventure."

"We have taken you to the *Past* and into the *Future*, but this has only been possible with the assistance of Orb. He is a *wizard bear* of great courage and patience, and it is with his help that we have been able to help you. Perhaps because of this evening's revelations, you both now understand how *HAVING FUN* is part of life."

Molly and Ben both looked at Dodl, Aura and Orb.

"We can't begin to express our gratitude and how much we value this adventure, and this experience," said Molly.

"It's been absolutely incredible," said Ben.

"How can we ever repay you?"

"You can repay all of us who live in The Magical World of Fingley, by paying more attention to your promises," said Orb.

"By only making promises that you can keep. Also, by remembering that these promises are ways in which all of you can HAVE *FUN*."

"Thank you ~ we will ~ we promise," said Molly and Ben.

"Thank you so much," continued Molly.

"But before we leave you, can I ask a question Dodl?"

Dodl looked intently at Molly, wondering what on earth she could possibly wish to know.

"I notice you have PURPLE PAWS and I was wondering, if there is a reason for that?"

Dodl smiled back at Molly.

"Indeed there is Molly, indeed there is. A very long time ago, Orb and I lived far, far away from here. In fact we used to live in the constellations you see in the night sky."

"As you are well aware now, Orb is a wizard bear and because of this he has the natural ability to travel through time."

"However, as I am merely his apprentice, I did not have that power."

"Therefore Orb granted me this gift, by allowing me to hold the special amethyst crystal and recite some magic words. I will simply say that this process did in fact turn my paws purple, enabling me to enter into dreams and help in the way that my name suggests."

"My name Dodl means…"

"Doing Ordinary Deeds Lovingly."

Molly smiled at Dodl's explanation.

"Oh, I see. Thank you. You have given us so much to think about for the rest of our lives. We will never forget you all."

"Quickly now! The dawn is about to break and you have much to do before Sam and the twins wake up," said Dodl glowing with enthusiasm.

Before Molly and Ben could answer, Dodl and Orb had taken their leave and both bears were once again sitting proudly upon Aura's back.

With no time for 'goodbyes,' the magnificent Pegacorn majestically left the ground and launched into the air, carrying Dodl and Orb far into the distance.

Soon, they were all just a distant speck in the sky.

As Molly and Ben watched them disappear, they stood for a moment longer in the front garden, trying to absorb everything they had just been through.

They quietly opened the front door to their home, slowly crept upstairs and took off their dressing gowns.

Feeling completely flummoxed by the whole evening's events, Molly glanced at the bedside clock.

"Look Ben, its four o'clock in the morning. Perhaps we can get a bit of sleep before the children wake up."

Feeling completely exhausted, Molly and Ben removed their dressing gowns and Ben took off his scarf.

"It's a good job we had these to keep us warm Molly," he said yawning.

They both pulled back the bed covers and cuddled up together, quickly falling into a deep sleep.

9

A Revelation

Buzz ~ buzz, buzz ~ buzz, buzz ~ buzz...

The bedside alarm sounded loudly! Sleepily, Ben reached out his arm from under the bed covers and switched it to *'snooze'*.

"Oh Molly, let's just have a few more minutes please. I feel so tired," he yawned.

Molly peeped from under the covers. "I don't think we can Ben, I have the twins to dress and feed. We must get ourselves organised. Sam will be asking us about the cottage today because remember, Mum told us how upset he was last night."

Ben moaned, but quickly realised he had to get up and make the tea for breakfast.

"Ok ~ I'm getting up Molly," he said sleepily.

He climbed out of bed and looked for his slippers. He found one of them, but couldn't see the other one. He got on his knees to look under the bed. There it was!

He sat back onto the bed and just as he was about to put his foot into it, he saw a little yellow card.

"Look Molly, what's this in my slipper?" He picked the card up, turned it over and read it.

It's a Dodl ... TO HAVE FUN

"Look Molly. Look at this," he insisted.

Molly stood up to put on her dressing gown and as she was tying the belt around her, she looked down on the floor. Immediately in front of her was a similar little card.

She bent down to pick it up, and as she did so, she turned the card over to read it.

It's a Dodl ... TO HAVE FUN

"How strange! We both have the same little card. Where on earth did they come from?"

They both sat on the edge of the bed in total confusion.

"You know this is amazing Ben," she said.

"Last night I had the funniest dream that I have ever had. I dreamt that a small talking bear came into our bedroom. He then took us both on an amazing adventure to see the Aurora Borealis. We rode on a magnificent golden winged Pegacorn named Aura and flew to the Olympic stadium where Sam was playing football for his team."

"He scored the winning goal and was named Man of the Match!"

"That's strange," said Ben. "I had a similar dream too. I dreamt that you and I along with two bears named Dodl and Orb, went to a magical world called Fingley and we visited a house called Cobblestones."

"There we met three other small bears and a fairy called Amber. From Fingley, we went to The Olympic Stadium and watched Sam play a brilliant football match where he scored the winning goal!"

"Somehow, we went into a Time-Tunnel with the two bears on the Pegacorn, and we saw Sam leaving school yesterday, running across the playing field on his way home."

"But surely it was only a dream ~ wasn't it?" Ben asked curiously.

Molly and Ben sat on the edge of the bed looking at each other.

Simultaneously, something caught their eyes as they looked at the dressing table stool.

There too was something strange!

It was a football rattle!

"How on earth did that get there?" Molly exclaimed.

"I've no idea. But somehow I don't think it was a dream at all Molly. I think it must have actually happened."

"Look at your card again, it's identical to mine."

Molly took the card from Ben and placed them side by side on the dressing table. Then she put the football rattle beside them.

"Come on Ben, it's getting late. We need to get dressed quickly and go downstairs. We'll have to talk about this later."

When Molly opened the kitchen door, Granny was already there dressed and eating her breakfast. The twins were sat happily in their high chairs eating some porridge.

"Good morning Molly," she said.

"I hope you managed to sleep well after such a late night. I've given the twins their breakfast and made a pot of tea."

"Thanks Mum," said Molly, planting a kiss on Jessica and Amy's cheeks.

"Yes, I slept well thank you Mum," replied Molly.

"But I had the strangest dream ever and I don't think it was just a dream at all."

"Well come and sit down and tell me all about it," said Granny as she buttered her toast.

So Molly sat down and began to tell her all about the fantastic dream that she and Ben had both experienced.

No sooner had she finished talking, than Ben walked into the kitchen too.

"I'm just telling Mum about the similar dreams that we had last night. Do you want to tell her about your dream?" asked Molly.

So Ben began to explain his dream too.

"Well dear, I can tell you one thing for sure; whether it was a dream or not, if you did spend more time with Sam and the twins *having fun*, it would certainly make a difference ~ to all of you."

"And if Sam eventually became a world famous footballer ~ well I'd be so proud of him."

Granny sat back in her chair and wiped her chin with her napkin. Just then the kitchen door burst open as Sam ran to greet his Mum and Dad.

"Morning Mum. Morning Dad!"

"I can't wait to tell you about the amazing dream I had last night. It was fantastic!"

"I dreamt I was a professional footballer and I'd been chosen to play in the World Cup. My shirt was number 9 which is my favourite number, and as I was waiting in the tunnel to walk onto the pitch, I heard the crowd shouting my name:

"SAM GREEN ~ SAM GREEN."

"I couldn't believe it and look what I found on my pillow just now," said Sam excitedly.

"I don't know how it got there and I don't really know what it means ~ do you Mum?"

Molly took the little card from Sam and looked intently at it.

"No," she gasped in disbelief.

"It couldn't possibly be ~ could it?"

She turned the card over and read…

It's a Dodl … TO HAVE FUN

Speechless, Molly passed the card to Ben.

"Do you know what?" said Ben.

"From now on, we're going to have lots and lots of fun." He then turned to Sam.

"And that starts right now Sam!"

"When you've eaten your breakfast, quickly go and brush your teeth and get dressed."

"We're all going to go to the cottage today, even if it is a bit late; better late than never!"

Molly smiled and looked at the little card in her hand.

"Thank you Dodl, thank you Orb."

"Thank you Fingley, thank you Aura."

"Thank you Amber," she said silently to herself.

"You know what Mum…"

"You're never too old to *HAVE FUN*!"

"Thank goodness for dreams, because sometimes they can be so real can't they and this is one dream that I'll never forget!"

"Me too Molly. It's certainly been an 'eye opener' for me," interrupted Ben, as he winked at Sam.

Granny looked at them all as they sat around the kitchen table, laughing at the 'coincidences' they had all experienced during the night.

With that she smiled a 'knowing' smile.

Grannies always know more than they admit to ~ don't they?

Fingley Glossary

Atlanticus

The vast ocean surrounding The Magical World of Fingley. Also home to Serena the Mermaid and the Dolphins.

Aura's Stable

Where Aura the Pegacorn is stabled and where Pegacorn riding lessons can be booked by appointment with Amber.

Badger Springs

A retreat where the curious badgers meet.

Bluebird Bay

On the West coast of Fingley Bluebirds fly high. They keep watch over the rowing boat that can take you on a day trip into Atlanticus.

Bumblebee Cross

The bumblebees gather nectar from the vegetable garden and create their delicious organic honey for all The Fingley Folk to enjoy.

Eco Houses

A hamlet of sustainable Eco Homes created by the Fingley woodsmen, complete with Sedum roofs.

Elf Creek

An enchanting home to Elgiva the invisible Elf and the Elfins; nestled by the slip stream to Atlanticus.

Grednor

The terrifying land to the North of Fingley inhabited by a gruesome tribe of trolls known as The Elbacs.

Hazel & Oak Wood

This is the home of Ozzy the Owl, guardian of the magical wood where the animals forage for food and the squirrels make their drays.

Pixileta Cove

A very special home to Skye and all the Pixie Folk. Be careful not to enter without invitation. You have been warned!

Rainbows End

A colourful and heart-warming community centre for all The Fingley Folk to meet and have fun with their visitors. The Fingley Bugle is written and printed here by Prof. Horatio Plenticus.

The Field of Dreams

A huge expansive land for Ecology and Sustainability.

Carefree Drive

Connecting Rainbows End and Cobblestones for a perfect carefree Bike Ride.

Cobblestones

Home to The Fingley Fairies, The Bears under the Stairs and of course Dodl Bear and Orb the Wizard Bear.
(Dodl's adventure stories are written here too!)

Crystal Cave

A special place for everyone to sit in quiet contemplation surrounded by amazing crystal walls. It also has an underground cavern too! The cave is also protected by Orb's mystical sword.

Daisy Mountain

The magical Daisyslip herb covers the slopes of Daisy Mountain. It is also the home of Ursula the Sorceress & Witch and lots of unusual companions.

Deer Valley Road

This is on The Field of Dreams where the deer love to sprint and play.

Dolphin Bay

Situated on the East coast of Fingley, the resident Dolphins breach the waves to frolic and play. Rowing boats can be loaned for an exciting day trip to see the Dolphins in their natural environment.

Rock Falls

Where the salmon leap on their journey to Atlanticus.

Swan Lake

A glistening, mystical and magical home to Avalon Guardian of Swan Lake and her cygnets.

The Boutique

The experts in recycling and the perfect place to browse and exchange your unwanted items.

The Filter Critter

An amazing 'gurgling' waste machine that cleans the water.

The Trading Post

A magical emporium for all things Fingley.

The Vegetable Garden

The perfect place to learn how to grow your own vegetables and exchange seeds.

Keep up to date with the happenings of

The Magical World of Fingley!

Turn the page for the

Community Edition of

The Fingley Bugle

Prof. Horatio Plenticus

EDITOR

The Fingley Bugle

SAM'S PARENTS VISIT FINGLEY!

MOLLY & BEN ARE THE 1ST PARENTS TO VISIT

We are delighted to have met Molly & Ben when they visited Fingley with Orb and Dodl recently. Molly tells us that she was very impressed with Cobblestones and its wonderful garden. They were both excited to have been shown the Aurora Borealis and couldn't believe how much fun it was Time Travelling with Orb and Aura our very own Pegacorn. Molly & Ben are looking forward to spending lots more time with their children and look forward to seeing us all again whenever they can. Sam has donated his football kit. See advert.

Horatio Plenticus – Editor

SAM TRIALS FOR WORLD CUP TEAM!

We are all waiting to hear news about young Sam and his forthcoming trials that will take him far into his football career.

He is about to showcase his footballing talent to the many Scouts who have been watching his progress. We all wish him well and know that he has a fabulous career waiting for him.

Horatio Plenticus, Editor

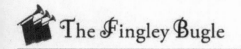
BRAIN TEASER

I absolutely *LOVE* puzzles and games... This time I thought I would create a Word Search based on Sam's story and his parents visit to The Magical World of Fingley. There are 15 words to find hidden within this puzzle. Enjoy!

Good Luck!
H. P

Future Awaits Word Search!

I	R	P	P	A	Q	Z	W	D	P	M	A	A	D	O
D	W	V	D	D	M	T	U	N	H	P	W	Q	J	Z
O	D	I	H	V	X	F	U	T	U	R	E	X	V	O
D	X	R	R	M	E	S	N	H	B	R	O	G	K	C
L	J	P	A	R	E	N	T	S	A	N	P	D	I	C
K	L	X	Z	A	H	Y	E	Q	M	F	Z	N	D	V
B	E	A	M	T	I	L	E	S	B	S	M	Q	L	A
Y	V	R	K	B	B	X	G	Q	E	E	F	T	P	D
S	A	F	U	N	Q	L	R	A	R	Q	U	B	W	U
O	R	Z	P	Q	Z	C	A	R	J	M	T	U	M	R
M	T	X	T	N	V	J	N	U	S	T	A	C	H	E
E	U	X	P	L	S	Q	N	A	H	W	N	F	R	G
D	V	G	G	F	S	Z	Y	Z	F	I	R	O	L	C
K	Z	X	U	R	Y	W	Z	D	R	N	C	X	S	C
Q	J	J	E	P	Q	H	K	W	O	S	Q	P	O	P
V	F	B	X	Q	A	V	L	S	U	H	R	X	Y	P
Q	A	G	Z	K	K	O	A	S	Z	X	G	P	M	U
F	I	A	G	F	R	G	F	O	O	T	B	A	L	L
B	C	C	O	T	T	A	G	E	Z	V	J	R	T	I
G	J	E	R	E	H	P	S	I	M	E	H	J	M	J

AURA	TWINS	GRANNY
TRAVEL	FUN	COTTAGE
PARENTS	SCORE	TILES
FUTURE	ORB	AMBER
FOOTBALL	DODL	HEMISPHERE

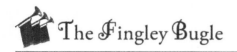

The Fingley Bugle

FOOTBALL FACTOIDS!

Did you know that:

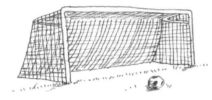

1

Football nets were not
introduced until the 1890s.

2

The first FA cup final
was in 1872.

3

Referees did not use
whistles until 1878.

4

The oldest existing football
club in the world is
Sheffield FC
- formed in 1857.

5

The ball used in professional
football has remained the same
size and shape for 120 years.

6

Nobby Stiles an ex World Cup
Player was so superstitious that
he used to wear the same
underpants for *every* match!

BRAIN TEASER

You have now read SAM'S FUTURE AWAITS!
Try this QUIZ to see how well you know Sam and everything Fingley!!!
There are 20 questions... Time Starts NOW!

Horatio's Top Tip:
Make sure to read
through the story,
Glossary &
Fingley Bugle to
answer the Quiz!

SAM'S FUTURE AWAITS QUIZ!

1. What are the names of Sam's twin sisters

2. What type of company does his parents own?

3. What are the names of Sam's parents?

4. What is Sam's favourite hobby?

5. What is the number on Sam's shirt?

6. What do Sam's parents experience on Aura?

7. What is the name of Sam's Geography Teacher?

8. What is Sam's school friend called?

9. What is Sam's ambition?

10. What is the design on Sam's duvet?

Turn over
for the final
questions!

SAM'S FUTURE AWAITS QUIZ CONTINUED...

11. What were the words written on the card that Sam found?

12. Who looked after Sam and his twin sisters?

13. Who is Prof. Horatio Plenticus?

14. Where does Dodl live?

15. Who is Queen of the Fairies?

16. What is the Pegacorn called?

17. What did Sam have to eat at the park?

18. What is the Crystal Cave protected by?

19. Who is Orb?

20. Who lives in Pixileta Cove?

ANSWERS:
Turn the book upside down to check your answers!

1. Amy & Jessica 2. Roof Tiles 3. Molly & Ben 4. Football 5. 9 6. The Aurora Borealis 7. Mr. Taylor 8. Greg 9. To be a famous footballer 10. Footballs 11. It's a Dodl to Have Fun 12. Granny 13. Editor of The Fingley Bugle 14. Cobblestones 15. Amber 16. Aura 17. Ice Cream 18. A Sword 19. The Wizard Bear 20. Skye

GET CREATIVE!

ARE YOU A BUDDING ILLUSTRATOR?

Send us your illustration/drawing of Dodl Bear!

Use: Any kind of coloured pens, pencils, felt tips or paints!

Send to: dodl@fingley.com

The most creative drawings will feature on the Official Website

www.Fingley.com

Get Set for... TIME TRAVELLING FUN!

The Magical World of
Fingley

TOM'S
TIME-TUNNEL QUEST

DAISA MORGAN

Dodl's Purple Paws & Magic Words,
Propel Tom Into His Exciting Future...

Adventurous, heart-warming, and fast moving,
Tom's Time-Tunnel Quest shows that each child, like Tom
is unique with their own dreams to fulfil...

WWW.FINGLEY.COM

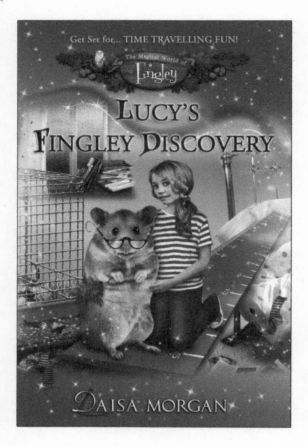

Get Set for... TIME TRAVELLING FUN!

The Magical World of
Fingley

LUCY'S
FINGLEY DISCOVERY

DAISA MORGAN

Doing Ordinary Deeds Lovingly,
Changes Lucy's Life Forever...

Funny, Inspirational and Magical!
Lucy's Fingley Discovery shows that having
responsibilities can be fun!

WWW.FINGLEY.COM

Get Set for... TIME TRAVELLING FUN!

The Magical World of

Fingley

AZIZA'S
BUBBLE ADVENTURE

DAISA MORGAN

A New World Is Waiting For Aziza,
She Just Doesn't Know It Yet...

Aziza's Bubble Adventure
is a rollercoaster ride, showing how being
friendly can make a difference!

WWW.FINGLEY.COM

My
Notes

My
Wishlist

I would That S more
Stay like milly.

Taryn Shrigley

Taryn Shrigley is an Illustrator, Designer and Multi Media Artist living in Derbyshire in the heart of England. She holds a Master's Degree in Visual Communications. Her achievements include a 'Designers and Art Directors' award for a series of book cover illustrations and designs produced for Penguin Books.

Taryn's digital artwork is inspired by Celtic Mythology, fairy tales and the Natural World. She views her computer stylus as her' magic wand' with which she creates fantasy worlds and characters. Her work has been published in magazines, as greetings cards, giftware and on C.Ds, DVDs and book covers.

She also illustrates children's books for the publishers 'Routledge', 'Jessica Kingsley, 'Taylor & Francis' and 'Open University Press'.

A Storybook World That's Brought To Life!

CHILDREN'S BOOKS | GIFTS | DODL BEAR®

Look out for your nearest
The Magical World of Fingley®
Official Stockist!

ᴅAISA MORGAN

Daisa Morgan is a Yorkshire-born Author and Creator of
The Magical World of Fingley®.

As a young girl she grew up reading traditional story
books admiring both Beatrix Potter and Enid Blyton. A
few years ago while having the experience of living in an
Eco-House in Scotland she began to 'scribble' down
ideas for children's books.

When Daisa returned to England she developed these
stories using a charming little bear named Dodl.

His name Dodl is an acronym for
'Doing Ordinary Deeds Lovingly'.

Daisa's intention is to create traditional stories for
primary school age children that are: Fun, Magical,
Educational and Inspirational.

*Encouraging children to fulfil their potential and
achieve their dreams.*

To organise a book signing or event please contact:
events@fingley.com
www.fingley.com